The Covid Test

Alok Jha

Ukiyoto Publishing

All global publishing rights are held by

Ukiyoto Publishing

Published in 2022

Content Copyright © Alok Jha

ISBN 9789359205328

All rights reserved.
No part of this publication may be reproduced, transmitted, or stored in a retrieval system, in any form by any means, electronic, mechanical, photocopying, recording or otherwise, without the prior permission of the publisher.

The moral rights of the author have been asserted.

This is a work of fiction. Names, characters, businesses, places, events, locales, and incidents are either the products of the author's imagination or used in a fictitious manner. Any resemblance to actual persons, living or dead, or actual events is purely coincidental.

This book is sold subject to the condition that it shall not by way of trade or otherwise, be lent, resold, hired out or otherwise circulated, without the publisher's prior consent, in any form of binding or cover other than that in which it is published.

www.ukiyoto.com

To,

My English Teacher, (Late) Mrs Swapna Saha

On a sultry April morning, the back porch of the bungalow, allotted to Chintamani Pandey, Deputy Commissioner of Excise, was resembling a war zone.

A woman in her mid-forties, who was of wheatish complexion and who had worn on her pink Palazzo a parrot green cotton tee, had positioned herself inside a white circle. Her brown-streaked hair was held loosely with a red band. A red mask in floral print had concealed much of her attractive features, with only a spot of vermilion showing where the middle parting of her hair was.

The woman alluded to above, who was also wearing white rubber gloves in her hands, was the better half of the Deputy Commissioner. In front of her stood a wrought iron table upon which grocery bags and two plastic baskets in red and blue were kept. A hand sanitizer was also lying on one end of the table.

With a frowning face, Mrs Pandey was taking out the contents of the bags and putting them in the baskets – fruits and vegetables in the red basket; rest into the blue one.

At a safe distance from his wife stood the Deputy commissioner, who was around fifty years of age, of medium height and lean muscles, his long face covered with a blue surgical mask. Upon his Olive Cargo shorts, he was wearing an Orange Printed Crew Neck T-shirt, the upper half of which was bathed in sweat.

After coming from the market, he had directly reached the back porch, where his wife had instructions to receive him in her safety gear.

He was presently supervising his wife's operation.

"Don't touch your nose with your hand," said the Deputy Commissioner.

"It's itching," the wife said, glaring at her husband.

"Then remove your gloves and sanitize your hands."

The wife, however, ignored the counsel, rubbed her nose lightly with her gloved hand, and resumed her work.

The Deputy Commissioner's eyes then fell on an elderly woman, of creamy white complexion, on whose shoulder-length black hair not a single strand of grey was visible. A little while ago, this picture of elegance had materialized on the verandah, wearing red-rimmed Cat Eye glasses, and with an iPhone 7 in her hand. She was the mother of the deputy commissioner who was christened Viveki Devi, some seven decades back.

She was looking at the proceeding on the ground with a disapproving eye.

"Mother, why aren't you wearing a mask?"

"I don't see why I have to wear one amongst people who are not infected with the coronavirus," the mother shot back.

"No use saying all that to him. He follows his own Covid Guidelines, and wants others to do the same. Look at the amount of veggies he has bought. Who is going to wash and cook all this? He stopped the maid from coming to our house even when the administration issued no such advisory."

Though the prime minister, in response to the pandemic, currently afflicting our living world, had announced a nationwide lockdown, these were the early days; so maids were not banned from coming to work.

The wife, who was sore about having to do all the household chores by herself, then picked up a strange-looking leafy thing, and asked, making a face, "What's this?"

For the first time a flicker of a smile appeared on the face of the Deputy Commissioner. He replied with the satisfaction of someone who has stumbled upon the solution of a vexing problem.

"It's called *Jungli Chauli*. A staple of the people in the tribal region. It's the reason why there are no Covid cases amongst them. Along with ginseng and garlic, *Chauli* is being touted as a possible cure for the virus".

The wife was not impressed.

She put aside the miracle plant. Then resuming her work, she said, "I am not going to cook it. You do it yourself. Anyway, I don't know how to make *Chauli*."

The Deputy commissioner looked at her in a slightly exasperated way, but, given her current mood, chose not to confront her.

When the Pandey couple was exchanging vital information on *Chauli,* the mother had opened her iPhone to verify some of the claims of her son.

Now armed with information, she confronted her son.

"Chintamani, your information is not correct. Of late, even the tribal belt is reporting daily cases of Covid. Ginseng or *Jungli Chauli* or for that matter any herb neither prevents nor cures Covid."said Viveki Devi.

"Who says?"

"WHO says."

"Who who?"

"WHO is an abbreviation for World Health Organization. It's a pity if you haven't heard about it," said the mother irritatingly.

"Oh that! I thought Hu was some Chinese charlatan. Mother, don't trust these Chinese. They are responsible for the virus."

The matriarch, however, ignored the Chinese angle. She said looking sharply at her son.

"I don't trust anything that is peddled as a cure for the virus."

Unable to meet the matriarch's piercing gaze, the son averted his eyes and looked in the direction of his wife, who had nearly finished distributing groceries in the two baskets. The only item remaining was a *Besan* pack, which she put into the red basket.

"No, no, no. That goes into the blue one. I have told you so many times that all packed items including potatoes and onions will be put in the blue basket and kept in the store room for two days before they are taken out for consumption."

The Deputy Commissioner had framed strict quarantine rules for grocery and any kind of violation irked him.

"But, today, I have planned to make *Kadhi*. How will I make one without *Besan*," the wife protested.

"You ought to have thought about it before. Make something else."

"Don't be unreasonable, Chintamani. After taking out *Besan*, she'd be throwing away the polythene pack. If at all the pack has been contaminated, the virus would be present on the polythene surface, and not inside *Besan*. There's no scientific evidence to suggest food items host the virus. Besides, I have never understood how isolating certain food items for two days will mitigate the danger of infection, when this virus is known to live on various surfaces for several days."

Unlike the Deputy Excise Commissioner, Viveki Devi possessed a scientific temperament. Though lacking in formal education, she was an avid reader. The propensity of the learned class to forward fake posts in WhatsApp groups had further aided her learning process. If a family member enthusiastically forwarded a History Post in the family group, revealing a hitherto unknown role of a national icon, she'd first google to verify the veracity of the piece; once enlightened, she'd right-swipe the said post and mark it as fake much to the displeasure of the member. Over the years this habit of correcting fake posts cutting across various disciplines of learning had put her on an equal footing with the educated members of her family.

The Deputy Commissioner was once left bristling when she challenged him on his home turf by flagging a fake post of his that poorly compared the performance of a previous government with the incumbent one on some economic indicators.

"Mother, please, we have already discussed this before. Let's not argue on this anymore."

The first hint that the matter was non-negotiable came from the wife. She threw the *Besan* pack back into the blue basket, picked up the red one, and casting an angry glance at her husband went inside the bungalow.

The matriarch, who was looking forward to a meal of *Kadhi* rice, was irritated by her son's inflexible stance. She made her displeasure known by retreating into her room.

Left alone, Chintamani called his daughter.

"Soni. Soni. Where are you?"

A girl just out of her teens, and brimming with excitement, appeared on the scene with a mask on her face and a mopper in her hands.

"Stay there. Don't come near."

As the daughter complied with the social distancing norm the father continued, "What were you doing?"

"Papa, I was on phone with Ajay *Mamu*. Did you meet him in the market today?"

The brother-in-law's mention brought a sour taste in his mouth.

"Silly fellow! He came from behind, covered my eyes, and asked me who he was."

"That was so funny. *Mamu* said that you jumped with fright." The daughter was laughing now.

"Stop laughing. Who does this in Covid times? He was not even wearing a mask. I had to tick him off for that."

"Papa, did you know *Mamu* and his friends had partied in Resort Mix-n-Mingle."

The Deputy Excise Commissioner in his illustrious career had raided the dens of many hardened bootleggers, but rarely experienced the shock which his party-going brother-in-law had just delivered to him.

Putting on the back burner his social distancing guidelines, he came close to his daughter and asked,

"Did you say Ajay partied with his friends? When did he do that?"

"A couple of days back. *Mamu* returned home last night. A risky adventure, but worth undertaking."

By faithfully reproducing the last line of her *mamu*, the niece endorsed her uncle's position on illegal parties.

"But how did they manage to party when all resorts are closed on account of the lockdown?"

"Trust *Mamu* to find a way out of legalities. Resort Mix-n-mingle is owned by an acquaintance of his friend. All his friends were there. Sort of a school reunion. *Mamu* called it "Party In The Time of Covid.""

Soni chuckled at her uncle's clever retitling of Garcia Marquez's classic.

However, the Deputy Commissioner, who had not developed his literary taste beyond the texts he was required to read in school, was not listening. His whole demeanour had changed. Now there were worry lines on his forehead, his bald head glistening with beads of perspiration.

So engrossed was he in his thoughts that his daughter had to remind him to collect the blue basket. As he picked up the basket and traced his way, first to the store room that lay in one corner of the back verandah, and then to the bathroom – the bathing ritual he had prescribed for himself required of him to rinse his body thrice with soap water – the daughter dutifully sanitized the areas he walked over with the mopper.

*****

The Deputy Commissioner's bungalow stood on several acres of land.

Over the years its many occupants had liberally used government resources to make several additions to its premises.

Presently, any visitor desiring a tour of the bungalow would have the luxury to see a lush green front lawn, a garden with a pond, mango and guava orchards, two garages, a tennis court, a cow shed and an outhouse. A paved road that ran on one side of the bungalow connected the portico with the garages.

Ever since the pandemic had struck, Chintamani was working out of the sparsely furnished outhouse. It had an attached bathroom, and was situated on the rear side of the bungalow, where the guava orchard was.

What had induced this shift in the workplace was his worry that office files brought by the peon may be the carriers of the virus. Also, he was of the opinion that if he conducted his meetings at the outhouse his family would be spared the risk of catching infection.

Presently, Chintamani was pacing outside the outhouse. After hearing from Soni that his brother-in-law had spent two days at Mix-n-Mingle resort, he was in the grip of fear. To give the matter further thought, he had come to the outhouse.

Silly ass! What a time and place he chose to party! The place is a Covid hotspot. It'd be a miracle if one came back from there without catching the virus. All his friends are like him, without a care in the world. What's the expression? Yes. Birds of a feather flock together. Met the whole lot of them during Ajay's marriage. Not one I can say with any degree of confidence who would have followed the safety protocol. Ah! Why would any conscientious chap attend a party in the first place!

Chintamani, who was feeling bitter, then minutely examined his fateful meeting with his brother-in-law in the market.

The idiot chose Covid time to play his guess-who game. All my fault, of course. Allowed him to take too much liberty with me. My nephew Abodh would never dare to do such a thing.

At this point he detected a silver lining.

But his bare hands touched only my eyes. My nose and mouth were covered with the mask. Don't think the touch lasted for more than thirty seconds; the fellow had removed his hands when I shrieked and shouted at him. After that, perhaps, for less than a minute he had stayed in close proximity, laughing and cheering himself by saying 'Jiju got scared. Jiju got scared'. Idiot…But that also means I may not have come into his contact for more than a minute. For, immediately after this, he was called away by the chap in front of whose car he had parked his bike. Bless the chap! I could leave because of him.

Just when the deputy commissioner had started to settle around the view that such a short duration posed no real threat of infection, he recalled reading the latest research on the virus: that the virus was perfectly capable of invading the body through the eyes; that the viral transmission was even more lethal in the event of a person coughing, laughing, or chatting – his brother-in-law guilty of doing the last two.

No sooner had the new epidemiological findings brought the dread back in Chintamani than he detected another silver lining.

It's possible he may not be infected. Should I wait for him to show symptoms? But it's equally possible that he may not show any symptoms. He is young. Goes to the gym. What's the term? Yes. He could be asymptomatic.

Normally, a rigorous thought process like this yields handsome results. But in Chintamani's case, it had started to not only wear him out, but also left him no wiser.

No use giving yourself false assurances. Assume he is infected.

He then contemplated taking a Covid test, but the very next moment baulked at his own suggestion.

These government hospitals are littered with Covid patients. No hygiene is maintained. Even if you are not infected you are sure to catch one the moment you go there.

In the end the only conclusion he could draw was to wait for the symptoms to show. Till then he decided to quarantine himself at the outhouse to save his family from a possible infection.

*****

When the world was fretting over this novel virus, the Deputy Commissioner's wife held the view that concerns about the virus were blown out of proportion. There was no reason to lose one's sleep over a few cases. In her estimation the effect of the virus was limited to metro cities. Barring the elderly and the sick, she thought, the virus was inefficacious for the vast majority. What gave strength to her view was the prevailing wisdom that the spicy diet made Indians immune to infection. Further, if at all these pathogens were around they were bound to perish in the scorching heat of the summer.

To an adherent of this school of thought, if you told that her brother was responsible for your quarantine, she'd be rightly outraged.

When the Deputy Commissioner broached the subject of his forced exile to his wife, and connected it to her brother's reckless ways, her outburst came. Already peeved with her husband for not allowing her brother to visit her during the lockdown, the wife told him that the virus was more in his head than in the environment. She also said that her brother was sensible and not reckless. If he thought there was even the slightest risk of catching infection, he wouldn't have gone.

It all ended with the wife telling her husband that if he chose to react in an exaggerated way it was his problem and not her brother's.

A miffed Deputy Commissioner then packed his clothes and toiletries and shifted to the outhouse.

The wife made no efforts to stop him. Ever since the lockdown was announced, he was breathing down her neck. He'd stand in the kitchen and insist on her cleaning the fruits and vegetables at least four or five times under the running water. If during this time she happened to venture into any part of the house he'd make her sanitize the entire area. Even if she went out to buy milk packets from the booth across her bungalow, he would not only force her to take bath but also make her rinse her clothes in warm water mixed with antiseptic. Every time anyone stepped into the house the floor would be mopped using a disinfectant.

Now with her husband staying away in the outhouse, she thought she'd get the much-needed reprieve from his incessant demands and supervision.

*****

It was late afternoon.

Chintamani was poring over office files which the peon had brought a few hours ago.

Since the announcement of the lockdown, his practice was not to pick up any file immediately but to let it remain untouched in a corner, especially earmarked for the purpose. He had read that on cardboard the coronavirus became ineffective after a few hours.

Just then the Deputy Commissioner saw the unmasked figure of Viveki Devi advancing in his direction. He immediately covered his face with a mask and rushed out.

"Mother, stop there. Don't come near," he screamed.

The matriarch, who appeared to be in an agitated mood, complied with her son's directive albeit grudgingly.

"Chintamani, what's this new drama of yours? Learned from *Bahu* that you have quarantined yourself."

Viveki Devi was taking her nap when the Deputy Commissioner had shifted his residence to the outhouse.

"You heard it right, mother. It's better to be safe than sorry, as the expression goes."

"Take that mask off, Chintamani. I am standing more than six feet away from you. Safe enough, even if you were carrying the virus."

The mother was irritated as she could not hear clearly her son's adage on safety.

The son complied with the directive, allowing her to continue.

"Yes, It was utterly reckless of *Bahu's* brother to have gone partying in these times. But that doesn't establish his getting infected with the virus."

"It doesn't establish either that he is not getting infected with the virus."

"In that case I'd get myself tested instead of taking shelter in the servant's quarter," promptly came Viveki Devi's barbed reply.

"Mother, surely, you have read about those harrowing tales of botched Covid test results! Someone who is declared positive learns to his horror that it's a false alarm when he gets himself tested again."

"I'd not form an opinion based on a few erratic results."

"But, Mother, you know well that they start treatment even before test results arrive."

"That's because the treatment protocol requires them to do so."

The pandemic was in its initial stage. Covid tests were administered only at select government facilities, which sometimes delayed the results by more than a week.

"Mother, whatever you say I am not going for any test. I have heard enough stories of several patients being packed in one room with a common bathroom, and left without any attending staff. They don't allow any family members. The food they serve is awful. Why, the other day Mr Sinha was saying how he landed up in ICU due to the negligence of the health staff."

"The fellow has himself to blame for it. His situation worsened because he neglected his fever for three days."

"Who told you?"

"I spoke to his wife. Luckily, she and her two daughters did not catch any infection."

"Mother, they say women enjoy some form of immunity against the virus."

"Chintamani, you know well my aversion for any unsubstantiated reports. Instead of sitting here and worrying endlessly about symptoms, I will advise you to get tested. Don't worry if they admit you. Abodh will ensure the best care for you."

Chintamani's nephew, Abodh, was in the Health department.

"I'd rather pull strings with my own contacts than trust him with the job. Both Abodh and Ajay are cut from the same cloth."

"Fine. Then use your own influence and get it done."

"No, mother. I have made up my mind to wait for a few days for any symptoms to show. Let's not discuss this anymore."

Viveki Devi shook her head in exasperation. She was about to leave when the Deputy Commissioner tried to engage her on a subject of his interest.

"Mother, did you know that a simple breathing test can tell if you have Covid or not."

"That nonsense has already been debunked, Chintamani."

The son's fascination for pseudoscience always irritated her.

"You seem to be watching a lot of The Lallitop."

The Deputy Commissioner's jibe was directed at the news channel that ran a special segment debunking fake posts circulating on social media.

"Better than acquiring knowledge through WhatsApp or Facebook," came the sharp retort from Viveki Devi.

She then left for the bungalow leaving her son speechless.

*****

In the next three days, not much worth record took place at the Pandey household.

The family was under instruction to not transgress the line, which the Deputy Commissioner had drawn using white paint at a distance of six feet from the entrance of the outhouse. The members were also told to leave all food items on the wrought iron table parked outside the outhouse. Though the wife had instructions to clean the Deputy Commissioner's utensils separately in hot water, she never carried out the injunction, and brazenly lied whenever her husband enquired about it.

Contrary to her expectations, the woman of the house did not receive much relief from her husband's exile. Every hour or so her phone rang; the husband demanding from her *Kadha* or juice of bottle gourd or just plain hot water. By the third day the wife was so irritated with phone calls that she did not charge her phone for a long time when the battery died.

Twice a day Viveki Devi presented herself outside the white line apparently to enquire about her son's well-being, but, in reality, she paid close attention to any symptoms. On the third day she was alarmed when she found Chintamani labouring for breath. However, he dismissed her concerns by saying that he had gone for a brisk walk in the garden.

The Deputy Commissioner himself had found nothing to worry about. Everyday he performed the breathing exercises – which his mother had dismissed as bunkum – and was happy to note that he could comfortably stop his breath for more than twenty seconds.

The trouble then really began on the morning of the fourth day.

The Deputy Commissioner was in the habit of taking a break from work around 10 to drink coffee. A while ago his wife had brought coffee in a thermos flask. After pouring the freshly-brewed coffee into a china cup, when he took a sip, he found the strong nutty aroma of coffee missing. The realization made his heart skip a beat; for, smell loss, he had read, was an unmistakable symptom of Covid.

Overpowered by fright, Chintamani repeatedly took his nose near the coffee cup to detect its smell. But all that he achieved was a scalded nose tip.

He then looked around for any object that could stimulate his olfactory organ.

The only objects worth smelling in the room were a jar each of cookies and dry fruits, a pair of bananas, and an apple.

If at this moment an admirer of the Deputy Commissioner was present at the outhouse, he'd have been disappointed to see his idol running from one object to another; sometimes picking up bananas to sniff, and sometimes thrusting his nose in the cookie jar to smell.

When the Deputy Commissioner could not clear the self-administered smell test, he rushed out in panic.

A thought then crossed his mind that the garden was the ideal spot to remove his fear of smell loss.

Immediately, he whisked himself there.

The Deputy Commissioner's garden was a floral fiesta of Jasmine, Gardenia, Rajnigandha, Dahlia, Bougainvillea, Hibiscus, Sunflower etc. He loved the waft of floral scent coming from the garden and would often go there after dinner to take a stroll.

His approach to sniffing flowers was roughly similar to the way he smelled cookies and dry fruits a while ago.

Dashing from one bloom to another, in no particular order, he tried to catch a whiff of their fragrance.

When neither the strong scent of tuberose nor the soothing fragrance of Jasmine stirred his olfactory organ, a shiver ran through his spine.

As he stood contemplating his next move, his gaze fell on Viveki Devi. She had then ventured into the garden to pluck flowers for the purpose of making an offering to the Deity.

"What are you doing here, Chintamani?"

"Oh! Mother, you! Did you say what I was doing here? Oh! Nothing. It got monotonous at the outhouse. So I came here to take a stroll."

Not the one to buy evasive replies, the matriarch came straight to the point.

"Why were you going around sniffing flowers?"

A man used to exercising his authority both at home and office is usually hopeless in inventing lies.

"Did you say sniffing flowers, Mother? No. No. I was just looking at them."

"You can savour their beauty from a distance as well?" Viveki Devi said, coming closer to her son.

The Deputy Commissioner then tried to change the subject.

"Mother, don't you think the blooms are wilting in the summer heat." When he stopped. It occurred to him that he could, indirectly, get his mother to confirm if his fear of smell loss was real or not. He resumed, saying, "Mother, these blooms smell sweet, right?"

"Indeed, they smell sweet!"

"I mean the Jasmine, and the purple blooms there," he said pointing at the wisteria. "It's so soothing around this time of the year."

"They are soothing all through the year."

The Deputy Commissioner was now wiping beads of perspiration from his forehead. However, he continued, "Mother, did you notice your hibiscus is in full bloom today. Let me pick some for you."

A little while ago, he had tried in vain to smell the hibiscus.

Handing over a few of the red flowers to his mother, he asked in a hushed tone, "Mother, do you like its smell?"

"I can decide only if it has any fragrance."

"Yes. Yes. I forgot. Their smell is nothing to speak of."

The Deputy Commissioner tried to cover up his gaffe through forced laughter.

"Chintamani, tell me the truth. Have you lost your sense of smell?" Viveki Devi asked in a voice touched with concern.

"No. No. It's not true."

If he had heard the expression, he'd have said that his olfactory organs were firing on all four cylinders.

He just added that he was fine and left.

*****

Late in the evening of the same day, Viveki Devi again moved herself to the garden area. She wanted to call her grandson, Abodh, the Health Department worker, about whom his uncle had earlier spoken of in less than glowing terms.

It was an ideal location to hold a confidential chat.

Lying in one corner, the garden was shielded from view from most parts of the bungalow.

After being made to put up with the recorded message on Covid in both English and Hindi, she was connected to her grandson.

"Tomorrow morning be here by 9. And don't forget to bring two sturdy men along."

The grandson burst into a cackling laughter.

"Stop squawking like a duck," reprimanded the grandmother.

"Dadi, from when have you started picking up tiffs that you need sturdy men to settle your scores."

"I meant attendants who can be relied upon to admit your uncle into the hospital."

"What? What happened to Uncle? Dadi, I am coming there immediately."

"No need to come now. And don't get hyper either. It's just that I suspect your uncle may have infected himself with the coronavirus. But like a stubborn mule he refuses to get himself tested."

"I see where my sturdy men come into the picture. You want them to use their brute force should dear Uncle refuse to cooperate. But, Dadi, how can you be so sure about Uncle's catching the infection?"

"I saw him sniffing flowers in the garden."

The grandson cackled again, inviting another round of censure from Viveki Devi.

"Told you not to laugh like that. You will rupture my eardrums."

"Dadi, if dear Uncle derives pleasure out of smelling flowers, allow the poor chap this harmless indulgence.

Better than twiddling one's thumb or shaking one's leg."

"I really admire your capacity for drivel. He was sniffing at flowers because he thought he had lost his sense of smell," Viveki Devi said angrily.

"Is that so?" He then added after a moment of reflection. "Look, Dadi, however much I want to join you on this project, I must still say no to your offer."

"May I know why?"

"Because Uncle still treats me like that kid who needs constant monitoring. The other day he upbraided me for posting a picture of mine in the family group in which I had struck Shahrukh Khan's signature pose in the middle of the road with my arms wide open. You know well that I cannot even discuss weather with him on an equal footing."

"If you are done with your pouring out of your woes, can I say something?"

"Yes, if you must."

"You will not barge into the house as his nephew. You will wear a disguise and pretend to be someone from the Health department, who has orders to take away a Covid-suspect hiding in the bungalow."

"Wow Dadi! You do your homework well! In disguise I can say things which otherwise I cannot even think of saying. Sample this: He, he, he. Chintamani Pandey, you thought you could give us a slip, and we'd not get a wink of it. You forget we can even recognise the wings of a flying bird." When he broke off and spoke in a dejected tone.

"But, Dadi, there's a lockdown. I won't be able to arrange stuff like a wig or a beard."

The matriarch, who was annoyed by her grandson's frivolous approach, replied, "You don't have to. Covid protocol requires you to wear a hooded coverall suit and face mask."

"Perfect," said the grandson, resuming his earlier exuberance. "I will tell you what…Should this Uncle of mine put up any resistance, which no doubt he'd, I shall be very firm in dealing with him. I'd be damned if after taking a stern line he isn't following me with a bowed head. Oh Dadi, I can't tell you how thrilled I am at the prospect of swapping my place with Uncle's." He briefly paused and asked, "Dadi, do you think I should get one of the attendants to video-shoot the whole thing for posterity."

Viveki Devi, who was patiently hearing him, and not liking it, now lost her temper.

"You will not do anything of that sort. You will certainly not utter those filmy dialogues. For God's sake don't overdo it, and curb your instinct to break into that irritating laughter of yours, lest you end up giving yourself away. Remember there's no margin for error."

"Have no worries, Dadi. You have just signed up for your job the most reliable man on the planet."

Viveki Devi disapproved of her grandson's bravado. She hung up saying, "Complete all formalities and come here in time. I do not want to put this off even for a day."

*****

Viveki Devi was not the type of manager who after drawing a plan takes a back seat and lets other players execute it.

She kept pestering her grandson with her phone calls till he got up from his bed, took his shower, and left home to fetch an ambulance. At one point he got so annoyed with her that he threatened to walk out of the assignment if her phone calls did not stop.

Presently, she was standing on the front verandah waiting for her grandson to come.

Mrs Pandey had gone to buy groceries while Soni had gone to get study notes from a friend.

Viveki Devi, who had prior information of their engagements, had deliberately kept these two out of her scheme.

Soon an ambulance came and stopped outside the bungalow. Three men in Covid gear got off it.

As they opened the gate and walked inside, the matriarch too stepped down the verandah, crossed the paved road that ran adjoining the portico and came into the front lawn to receive them.

In the Hindi cinema of the seventies, the hero, after receiving an SOS from the distressed villagers, would come riding on a horse, overcoming all barriers, hold the hands of the village elder and say, 'Baba I have come. Now, you need not worry. I will deliver you from the sins of the *Jamindaar*.'

(It's a different matter that in the very next scene the *Jamindaar's* henchmen would make the hero fall from his horse, tie him with ropes, and present him before their master. Before the hero was able to honour his word, much action would pass, including a sequence, in which just when the hero appeared to be gaining an edge in his fight with the *Jamindaar*, hero's sister or mother would appear from nowhere, and pass the edge back to the *Jamindaar* by letting him take her hostage.)

Much in the same vein, one of the three Covid warriors came forward, held Viveki Devi's hands and delivered the filmy line, "Dadi, I have arrived. Now, you need not worry. Tell me where your son is hiding."

In the just narrated scene of the Hindi Cinema a typical response of the village elder would be, 'Son, now you are our only hope.'

However, Viveki Devi, who had an aversion for anything cinematic, jerked her hands from the man, walked to the tall, slender chap at the back and remarked with a frown on her face.

"What's this tomfoolery about?"

"*Dadi*, you recognized me?"

The disbelief in the grandson's voice was then replaced with concern.

"In that case, let's call off the whole thing. Uncle is certain to see through the subterfuge."

"What nonsense! I was able to recognize you only because the other two do not match you in height. Besides, you ought to have the sense to send someone who could mimic you."

"You are right, Sherlock Holmes."

"Who is this Holmes?"

"A fictional character who used his uncanny powers of observation and reasoning to solve crimes."

Viveki Devi, who was focussed on the task at hand, ignored the comparison.

Together they began walking towards the outhouse, the two attendants following suit.

"What's Uncle's mood like? Is he in one of those states in which he taught us Maths."

"How does that matter? You aren't here as his nephew. Be in your character. Now hush up."

The matriarch though of formidable mental constitution was feeling the tension build up in her.

*****

When Abodh arrived with his troop, he found his uncle ensconced on a white plastic chair, reading newspaper.

"Mr Chintamani Pandey?" Abodh said, disguising his voice.

"Chintamani Pandey, indeed."

Surprised to see the three hooded men, the Deputy Commissioner had gotten up from his chair.

The matriarch who had let the three men take charge was hidden from view.

"My name is Shahrukh Khan. We have come from the State Health department."

As Chintamani eyed him suspiciously, it occurred to Abodh that, perhaps, he ventured too far by using the alias of a famous Bollywood superstar. He quickly resumed his serious tone.

"We have come to know that despite showing Covid symptoms you have not reported yourself to the department."

"Who says?"

"We have it from a credible family source," said Abodh, not sure whether or not to name his grandmother.

"That family source will have a name!"

"I called them." Viveki Devi now said coming from behind.

"Mother, you got them here? I just can't believe this. But why?" The Deputy Commissioner asked, shock written all over his face.

"Because you left me with no choice."

"Mr Khan, I think there has been some misunderstanding. I can assure you that no one suspected of Covid has taken refuge here."

"There's no misunderstanding. He is your patient. Take him away." The matriarch said agitatedly.

"One minute. Let me handle this." Abodh tried to impose his authority on the warring sides.

"Is it not true, Mr Pandey, that you have quarantined yourself here in the servant's quarter?"

"Yes. True. But…"

Before the Uncle could explain the circumstances that brought him to the outhouse, the Nephew interrupted him.

"Is it also not true that you were sniffing at flowers because you feared you had lost your sense of smell?"

"Hmm…But then my fears were dispelled when I smelled cow dung."

"What? You smelled cow dung?"

Saying this, the nephew cackled. Before his signature laughter could ring alarm bells in her son, Viveki Devi pinched her grandson's hand to warn him.

"I mean you could have smelled turmeric or any of the strong-smelling spices. Why cow dung? Do you often smell cow dung?"

"I didn't choose to smell cow dung. I stepped on it accidentally. While trying to remove the stain from my slippers I realized I could smell its strong stench," The Deputy Commissioner said, suppressing his anger.

"He is lying. The same evening I saw him summon a quack."

"Mother, the man whom I called is not a quack."

"Hold on, Chintamani. Are you aware that by engaging with quacks, you are posing a grave threat to your own wellbeing, and to that of your family. If responsible citizens like you promote unscientific temperament, what can we expect from the lower order."

"Will you stop talking, and take him away?" The grandmother was losing patience over her grandson's dilly-dallying.

"I am not going anywhere." The Deputy Commissioner had a ring of finality to his tone.

"Enough, Chintamani Pandey! You will have to come with us to the hospital. If you resist we will charge you with obstructing a government officer from doing his duty. You have already committed the offense of not reporting to the authorities under Epidemics Diseases Act, 1897."

The two attendants whose patience was growing thin interpreted their boss's threat as an order and moved swiftly, each taking hold of an arm of the Deputy Commissioner.

The bravado that the Deputy Commissioner was displaying until now had dissipated. For the first time he sensed the fear of being whisked away by these two burly men. Seized with fear, he started shouting and screaming at his captors and his nephew, threatening them with dire consequences.

But, when in response the two attendants tightened their grip on him, the Deputy Commissioner did something unexpected. He kicked one of his captors on the shin, and dealt a nasty blow on the ribs of the other with his elbow.

The immediate impact of this unexpected aggression was that the attendants set him free.

Capitalizing on his freedom, the Deputy Commissioner then turned and ran towards the front of the bungalow. As if, on cue, one of the attendants went after him.

The other attendant, who had received a blow on his ribs, was about to follow suit, when the matriarch warned him.

"Just stop him from fleeing the bungalow. Don't cause him any injury."

"*Maaji, Saheb* has violent tendencies. We can no longer afford to go soft on him," saying this, he ran to aid his colleague capture the Deputy Commissioner.

Viveki Devi and her grandson too walked a few paces to a spot from where the main gate was visible.

As they stood watching the spectacle of attendants chasing the Deputy Commissioner, the nephew offered an insight into his uncle's combative skills.

"I suppose all this belligerence comes from dealing with those bootleggers and history-sheeters."

The comment met an angry glance from Viveki Devi. She was annoyed at the way the script was unfolding.

Meanwhile, the Deputy Commissioner had reached the finishing line on the gate.

Before he could open the gate and flee, he realized one of the attendants had considerably narrowed the lead. Any attempt to escape was now fraught with consequences.

What had hampered his run was the type of footwear that he was wearing for the occasion. Not that he had any choice in this matter.

At the time the troop had announced in, the Deputy Commissioner was wearing sandals. Since there was not enough time to replace them with running shoes, he ran in them.

Meanwhile, the Deputy Commissioner had turned and dashed towards the velvety lawn.

By the time his chasers could make sense of his unexpected move, the Deputy Commissioner disappeared into that side of the bungalow that had tennis court and garden.

If a commentator had gone live at this moment, he would certainly have remarked that it was a good strategic move. Not only was the vast stretch of land ideal for a run-and-chase sequence of this nature, but it also gave the Deputy Commissioner an advantage of being on familiar terrain.

Taking note of the shift in the venue, the two spectators began walking towards the back porch from where they hoped to catch a glimpse of the action.

"*Dadi*, I am telling you, if Uncle's strategy is to tire my men by running around the trees and the pond, he's in for a surprise. These two are the best of the lot. Tailor-made for a job of this nature. Ever since Covid struck, they have seen a fair amount of action. One of them, I am told, had earned his spurs chasing wild boars in paddy fields."

"Stop blathering, and go and see what they are up to. See they don't harm Chintamani in any way."

After despatching her grandson, Viveki Devi, who had recently gone through a bypass surgery, followed him at a slow pace.

The garden area was populated with tall and dense trees. The terrain was so uneven that even the small pond, which was at the centre of the garden, was hidden from plain view.

When Abodh reached the back porch, it was a particularly slack moment in the chase sequence. The wily uncle had managed to fox the two runners. One of them acutely felt the lack of intimate knowledge of the terrain when he slipped into the pond.

No sooner had Abodh chosen a vantage point to watch the proceedings than his eyes spotted a baby monkey. Presently, this native of the garden area was squatting on the wrought iron table, which the readers would recall, was used earlier to host groceries.

Being a frequent visitor of the bungalow, Abodh was on pally terms with this baby monkey. To exchange pleasantries with his simian friend, he had come up with a unique method.

Using a banana as a bait, he'd first tease the monkey and when he had his fill of entertainment, reward it with the fruit.

In the absence of a bait, Abodh picked up a twig and dangled it in front of the baby monkey. The monkey, who could clearly tell a banana from a twig, was not impressed by this act.

Abodh repeated the trick a couple of more times. When he failed to attract the monkey's attention, it occurred to him that the monkey was unable to recognize him because of his Covid gear.

To let the monkey see his face clearly, an enlightened Abodh then removed his mask and shades.

The familiar face stirred the monkey to act. Before Abodh could realize, it had ripped apart his face shield and snatched his shades, leaving his face open to plain view.

The enormity of the goof-up dawned on Abodh when he heard his uncle scream his name who, after managing to give his chasers a dodge, was catching his breath a little distance away from the back porch.

When Abodh was at school, he once tried to regale his classmates by mimicking their science teacher who spoke with a nasal twang. All the while he was performing on the podium he was unaware that one of his audience included the science teacher who was then standing outside the classroom.

The fear which he experienced then was similar to what he was going through now.

As he stood frozen on his spot, his uncle came around him, both anger and disbelief showing on the Deputy Commissioner's face.

"So it's you who lent a helping hand to mother. I should have thought so. But for your active participation mother could never have pulled out this criminal conspiracy."

The Deputy Commissioner looked angrily at his mother, who was standing nearby, and had witnessed the monkey reveal her grandson's identity.

"Uncle, please…"

"Shut up! Your irritating laughter did ring a bell, but I thought no more of it."

"Uncle, sorry! But it was not my fault. It was *Dadi's* idea." Abodh looked helplessly at Viveki Devi, and added "*Dadi*, why don't you say something."

Before she could plead his innocence, the Deputy Commissioner's piercing cry came.

"Shut up! You ought to have the sense to say no to her. If she asks you to jump into a well, will you do it."

"No, Uncle."

The Nephew had no difficulty in answering this question. As a child, he was often asked by his uncle, if on other's prodding, he'd consider the possibility of taking a leap into the well.

However, the Uncle was not impressed by his answer.

"You had the gall to speak to me in that high-handed manner and stand and watch those scoundrels chase me all around the bungalow!"

The Uncle, who was frothing at the mouth, forgot to add to his list of charges, the Nephew's impudence in using the moniker of Shahrukh Khan.

While the Nephew chose to remain mum at the charges, the scoundrels alluded to in the speech showed up. The delay in their arrival had resulted from a combing operation, which the attendants were carrying out in the garden area after they suspected the Deputy Commissioner of hiding behind the hedges.

When the attendants saw their boss shivering in front of their prized catch, they realized the sport had been called off.

Meanwhile, the matriarch, who was still feeling bitter about the missed opportunity, addressed her son.

"The attendants had no burning desire to chase you. If you had gone with them for the test none of this would have come to pass." She then cast a glance at her grandson, and added, "It was all my fault to recruit him in the first place. If I had involved the monkey, it'd have done a better job than him."

"Bless the monkey, who had more sense than him and foiled your scheme!" The Deputy Commissioner said sarcastically.

Abodh used the spat between the mother and the son as an opportunity to mend fences with his uncle.

"Err, Can I say something?" As Abodh looked expectantly at his audience, he discerned hostility in their glances. Nevertheless, he continued, "*Dadi*, it now seems you did not sufficiently examine the evidence while drawing your inference of Uncle catching the virus. The empirical evidence that has just come up strongly refutes your theory. An infected person, low on immunity, will not be able to sprint for so long. Think about it." Momentarily forgetting his own role in the messy affair, he added, "On the flip side, Uncle put up a commendable performance in giving these two seasoned runners a run for their money."

One of the attendants still regretting the timing out of the contest jumped to defend himself.

"If we had not lost precious time getting ourselves acquainted with the geography of the place, we'd have pinned him down in no time."

It was true. The Deputy Commissioner had the advantage of playing the match on home turf. But, instead of conceding this point, he shouted at the attendants

"Shut up! If my own nephew wasn't involved in this stupidity, I'd have seen to it that you were discharged of your responsibility." Then turning to his nephew, he barked, "Tell them to leave the premises at this very moment."

The nephew signalled the duo to leave. After they left the Deputy Commissioner continued, "You should be ashamed of your conduct. If I were in your place, I'd have drowned myself in pint-sized water."

"Stop shouting at him. Whatever you have to say, you say to me."

The grandmother now came fully to her grandson's defence.

"I wish I could say something to you, Mother."

The Deputy Commissioner made no attempt to conceal his sarcasm.

Around this time Mrs Pandey who had gone grocery-shopping made an appearance.

Initially, she had lost her nerves when she saw the ambulance parked outside the bungalow. However, she was subsequently put at ease by the two attendants who left no details in briefing her about the messy affair.

Relieved to see his aunt, Abodh promptly came forward to touch her feet. After blessing him to live for ages, she directed her frustration at the matriarch.

"Ma, what was the need to call these health workers? You know well how your son is. His reactions are extraordinary even on issues that are trivial in nature."

"When he summoned the quack, I was certain that he had caught the virus. I was worried that his foolish reliance on herbs and home-grown methods would only worsen his situation."

Peeved at the charges levelled by the two women, the Deputy Commissioner first addressed his mother.

"I have said this before. He is not a quack. There are many who'd attest to his enviable knowledge of herbal medicine." Then turning to his wife, he added, "My reactions aren't over-the-top. I carefully weigh the pros and cons before I respond to any crisis."

"Provided the crisis has some rational basis. One doesn't quarantine himself merely on the basis of a suspicion," retorted the better-half. She then took a deep breath and said, "When I was in the market I received a call from Ajay. A few days back someone in his bank had tested positive. So the bank manager got everyone tested for Covid. My brother's report is negative. She added looking scornfully at her husband, "From day one I knew his fears were unfounded."

Though the Deputy Commissioner was relieved to hear this news, he did not show any emotion on his face. That part was left for the matriarch, who sent a silent prayer of gratitude to God.

She then turned to her son and asked, "But why were you sniffing at the flowers if you had not lost your sense of smell?"

"For a brief while all evidence did point in that direction."

The Deputy Commissioner omitted any reference to the embarrassing episode of smelling cookies and dry fruits.

"But were you able to detect any smell in the flowers?" A curious Viveki Devi repeated her question.

"No."

"No?"

"The flowers that we have in the garden area either do not give out any smell or smell only at night," said Mrs Pandey matter-of-factly.

"Uncle, it's not uncommon to experience episodes of loss of smell or shortness of breath, when one is stressed or anxious."

Even though the nephew had spoken out of turn, he was not reprimanded by the uncle.

"Yes. That seems to be a plausible explanation," said Viveki Devi.

If she was half-convinced by the daughter-in-law's reply, the grandson's explanation removed any trace of doubt in her.

Ideally, Abodh would have liked to celebrate such a news with loud expressions of joy and relief, with all parties teasing his uncle for blowing up a minor issue, and the Uncle himself gracefully participating in the banter with statements like, 'Oh what a fool I have been. Dug up a mountain only to find mice,' and it all ending with the Aunt inviting everyone for a breakfast of stuffed *Parathas*.

But, seeing the non-celebratory mood of the gathering, Abodh kept his statement succinct.

"All's well that ends well. Everything is well with the world and the God in his heaven is smiling." When that failed to elicit even a chuckle, he said, "Err, I am leaving now."

"You are not going anywhere. I am still not done with you," came the booming voice of the Uncle.

As Abodh looked helplessly, the Aunt came to his rescue.

"Let him go. He came in the ambulance. God knows how many Covid patients it must have ferried."

The shrewd woman's psychological play cleared the way for Abodh. The Deputy Commissioner immediately left for the bungalow.

As Mrs Pandey winked at her nephew, he smiled and thanked her. Heaving a sigh of relief, Abodh then began walking towards the exit.

*****

About the Author

Going against the grain of prevailing wisdom, this writer decided to join the unfortunate tribe of Screenwriters of Hindi soap operas and, for nearly two decades, helped fictional mothers-in-law scheme against their docile daughters-in-law.

During lockdown two incidents so assaulted his peace of mind – otherwise, a creature of placid waters – that to restore his sanity, he decided to write this book.

In the first incident, an insurgent group of neighbourhood pigeons, keen to reclaim the balconies of his suburban flat, had begun despatching two intruders daily through the gaps in pigeon nets. Since his Stoic upbringing prevented him from taking any retaliatory action, he was forced to help the avians find their way back to their handlers.

In the second, his friends and acquaintances, who had added him in their WhatsApp groups, without taking his consent, and often in the wee hours of the day, had started posting messages that contained irrefutable cure for the virus.

Readers, be warned. He has no intention of leaving you with this book alone. More are in the offing, each promising to be funnier than the previous one.

www.ingramcontent.com/pod-product-compliance
Lightning Source LLC
LaVergne TN
LVHW041639070526
838199LV00052B/3453